S0-CQQ-738

Fact Finders®

NASTY (BUT USEFUL!) SCIENCE

FARTS, VOMIT,
and Other Functions That
HELP YOUR BODY

by Kristi Lew

Consultant:
Michael Bentley
Professor of Biology
Minnesota State University, Mankato

Franklin Library
Summit Public Schools

CAPSTONE PRESS
a capstone imprint

Fact Finders are published by Capstone Press,
151 Good Counsel Drive, P.O. Box 669, Mankato, Minnesota 56002.
www.capstonepub.com

Copyright © 2011 by Capstone Press, a Capstone imprint.
All rights reserved.
No part of this publication may be reproduced in whole or in part, or stored in a retrieval system,
or transmitted in any form or by any means, electronic, mechanical, photocopying, recording,
or otherwise, without written permission of the publisher.
For information regarding permission, write to Capstone Press,
151 Good Counsel Drive, P.O. Box 669, Dept. R, Mankato, Minnesota 56002.
Printed in the United States of America in North Mankato, Minnesota.

032010
005740CGF10

 Books published by Capstone Press are manufactured with paper
containing at least 10 percent post-consumer waste.

Library of Congress Cataloging-in-Publication Data
Lew, Kristi.
Farts, vomit, and other functions that help your body / by Kristi Lew.
 p. cm.—(Fact finders. Nasty (but useful!) science)
 Summary: "Describes the science behind body functions that keep people
alive"—Provided by publisher.
 Includes bibliographical references and index.
 ISBN 978-1-4296-4539-3 (lib. bdg.)
 1. Human physiology—Miscellanea—Juvenile literature. I. Title. II. Series.
 QP37.L43 2011
 612—dc22   2009050345

Editorial Credits
Jennifer Besel, editor; Matt Bruning, designer; Eric Manske, production specialist

Photo Credits
Capstone Studio: Karon Dubke, 21, 29 (ear wax), 29 (sweat); iStockphoto: DNY59, 13, Harun Aydin, 23
(skeleton), idris esen, 24, Sebastian Kaulitzki, cover (organs); Photo Researchers, Inc: John Bavosi, 9,
P.M. Motta & F. Carpino/Univ. "La Sapienza", 11, SPL, 19 (cell), Steve Gschmeissner, 27; Shutterstock:
Andrea Danti, 17, James Klotz, 29 (spit), Jamie Wilson, cover (algae), Kevin Lepp, 29 (vomit), Leigh
Prather, 5 (waxy goo), Lorelyn Medina, 23 (lungs), Ralf Hirsch, 19 (wound), Rob Byron, 29 (urine),
Sebastian Kaulitzki, 5 (human organs), 15, 29 (organs), Tischenko Irina, 5 (liquid), Ultrashock, 5 (muddy
splash), Ultrashock, cover (mud)

Artistic Effects
iStockphoto: Dusko Jovic, javarman3; Shutterstock:belle23, cajoer, Hal_P, krupinina, Pokaz,
Ultrashock, xiver

TABLE OF CONTENTS

AMAZING BODY

The human body is an amazing machine. Your lungs take in a gas called oxygen. Then your heart pumps oxygen-filled blood through your body, keeping you alive. At the same time, other organs are taking care of the food you eat. They break down food into chemicals your body uses for energy. The human body is a stunning system, isn't it?

But the human body can be gross too. It oozes liquids. It gives off stinky smells. It makes all kinds of sounds. But as nasty as they may be, all of these bodily functions have a purpose. Let's take a closer look at some of the disgusting, but helpful, jobs of the human body.

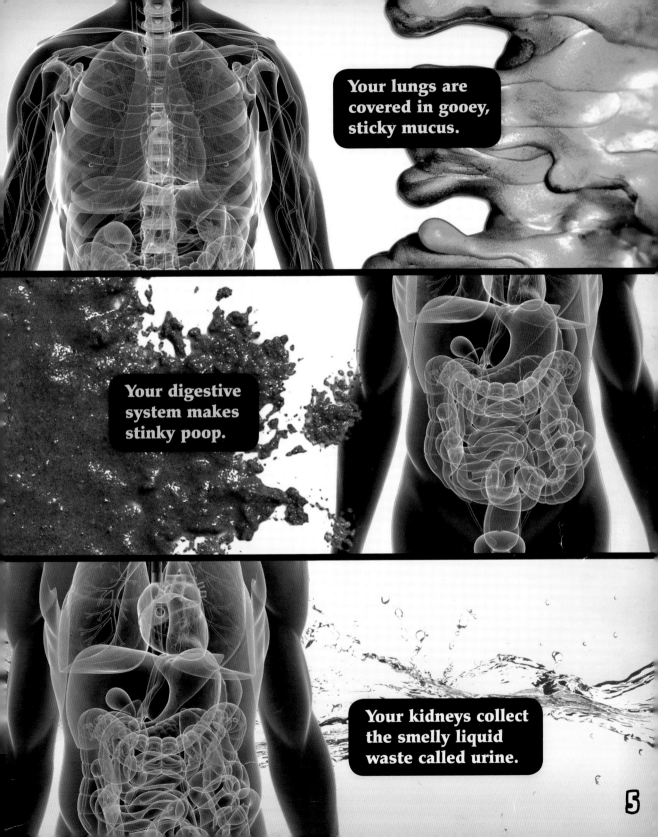

Your lungs are covered in gooey, sticky mucus.

Your digestive system makes stinky poop.

Your kidneys collect the smelly liquid waste called urine.

UP IT COMES!

Vomiting is one of your body's nastier functions. There are several reasons why your body might eject what you've eaten. One reason is that your body has been invaded by harmful **microorganisms**. Most of these critters are helpful to our bodies. But a few of them, like viruses and some bacteria, make your body sick. Poisons or some medicines make you sick too.

Your body is on guard for harmful substances. Cells called **chemoreceptors** are the guards. If they detect a poison, they send out an alert. These cells send a message to a part of the brain called the chemoreceptor trigger zone. The trigger zone passes that message on to the vomiting center in your brain. The vomiting center then sends out the command—get rid of it!

microorganism: a living thing too small to be seen without a microscope

chemoreceptor: a cell that tells the brain if poisons are in the body

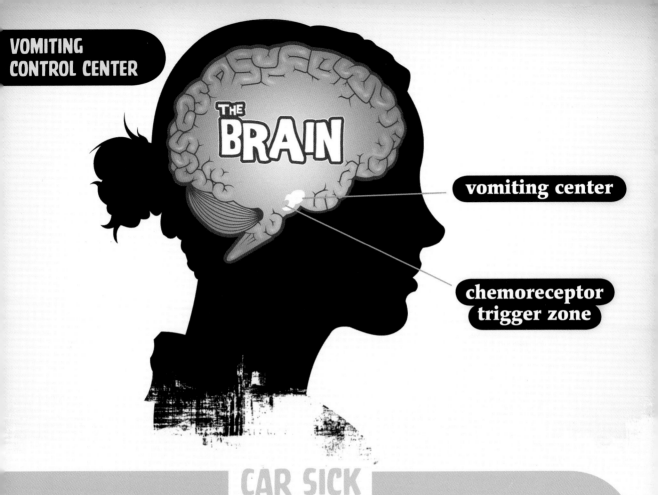

THE BRAIN

vomiting center

chemoreceptor trigger zone

CAR SICK

Motion sickness can cause you to vomit too. Your brain gets constant reports about what you're doing from different parts of your body. If you're in a moving car, your inner ear, muscles, and skin tell your brain that you're moving. But if you're reading at the same time, your eyes tell your brain you're sitting still. To your brain, this disagreement spells trouble. Your brain handles the trouble by making you hurl. Some scientists think that when you have motion sickness, the brain believes you've been poisoned. The brain orders your body to lose your lunch to get rid of the poison.

So how does your body get food to come back up? First, your brain tells the muscles in your abdomen to tighten. This action squeezes your stomach, causing the pressure in your stomach to go up. In the stomach, a slimy mix of food and digestive juices push against a muscle in your **esophagus**. When the pressure gets to be too much, the muscle relaxes. Puke is projected up your esophagus and out of your mouth.

FOUL FACT

Watching someone else puke can trigger your body's vomiting reflex. Your brain wants to make sure you don't have whatever is making the other person sick.

esophagus: the tube that carries food from the mouth to the stomach

HOW YOUR BODY VOMITS

1. The brain sends a signal to the abdominal muscles.

2. The abdominal muscles squeeze the stomach.

3. Food and juices in the stomach push against the esophagus muscle.

4. The muscle relaxes, and puke pushes up the esophagus and out the mouth.

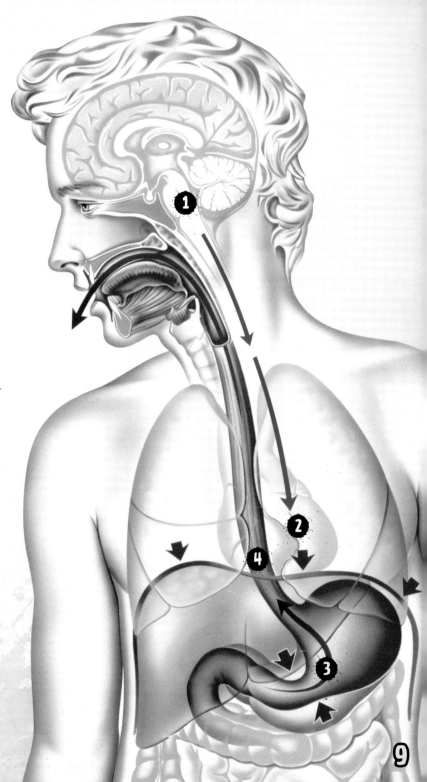

9

PASS THE GAS

Food and drinks aren't all you gulp down when you eat. You swallow air too. And if you drink soda, you swallow another gas called carbon dioxide. All that air and gas builds up in your stomach. When the organ can't hold it in anymore, the gas pushes up through your esophagus. It escapes through your mouth as a burp.

Farting is also caused by escaping gas. These backfires are caused by gas made while your food is being **digested**. While some types of bacteria make you throw up, other types help your body digest food. They break food into vitamins, minerals, and other nutrients that your body needs. But in the process, these bacteria also produce gas. Your body needs to get rid of the gas. When too much gas builds up in your large intestine, it comes out through your backside.

digest: to break down food so that it can be used by the body

intestinal wall

bacteria

FOUL FACT

The average person needs to get rid of about 1 quart (1 liter) of gas a day. Most people burp or fart at least 10 to 15 times a day.

You've probably noticed that some farts are more stinky than others. Bacteria create a mixture of gases, including hydrogen sulfide. This gas really stinks up the place. Hydrogen sulfide also gives rotten eggs their nasty smell.

GOTTA GO

Peeing is another way your body gets rid of stuff it doesn't need. During digestion, chemicals called enzymes break down **nutrients** from food into smaller chemicals. These chemicals are sucked into your bloodstream. Once in the bloodstream, they travel through the body. Your body's cells use the broken-down nutrients to make energy.

But not all the liquid and nutrients in your food are needed. Your kidneys take extra vitamins, water, salt, and chemicals out of the bloodstream. This mixture of waste chemicals and water is called urine. Urine drains out of your kidneys into your bladder. Your bladder stores the urine until you can find a bathroom.

FOUL FACT

On average, a person pees out 1.5 quarts (1.4 liters) of urine every day.

nutrient: a substance needed by a living thing to stay healthy

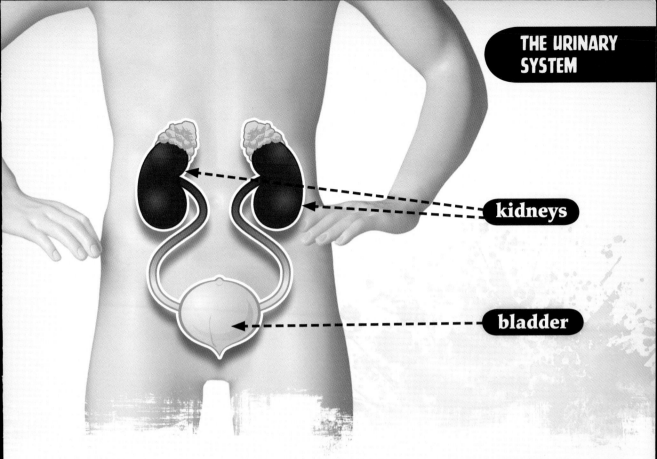

kidneys

bladder

A WEE BIT ABOUT PEE

What gives pee its pretty yellow color? A chemical in your small intestine called bile does that for you. Bile helps the body digest food. As you digest food, the bile is broken down and creates different **pigments**. One of those pigments is yellow. The kidneys filter the yellow coloring out of the bloodstream. The coloring goes into the urine mix and makes pee yellow. A different bile pigment gives poop its lovely green and brown shades too.

pigment: a substance that gives color to something

13

THE POOP SCOOP

Fruits, vegetables, and other plants contain fiber. Fiber can't be broken down by the digestive system, so it doesn't go into the bloodstream. It continues down the digestive tract until it reaches the end—the large intestine. This undigested food is part of what forms poop.

There are other things in poop too. Poop has water in it. It also has bile and bacteria. Bile gives poop its color. Bacteria munch on poop, releasing chemicals that give it a foul smell.

In the large intestine, solid waste gets formed into tube-shaped poop. Two muscles at the end of the large intestine keep the waste from just dropping out. As more waste builds, the pressure in your intestine tells you it's time to go to the bathroom. Only when you relax those muscles does the waste empty out.

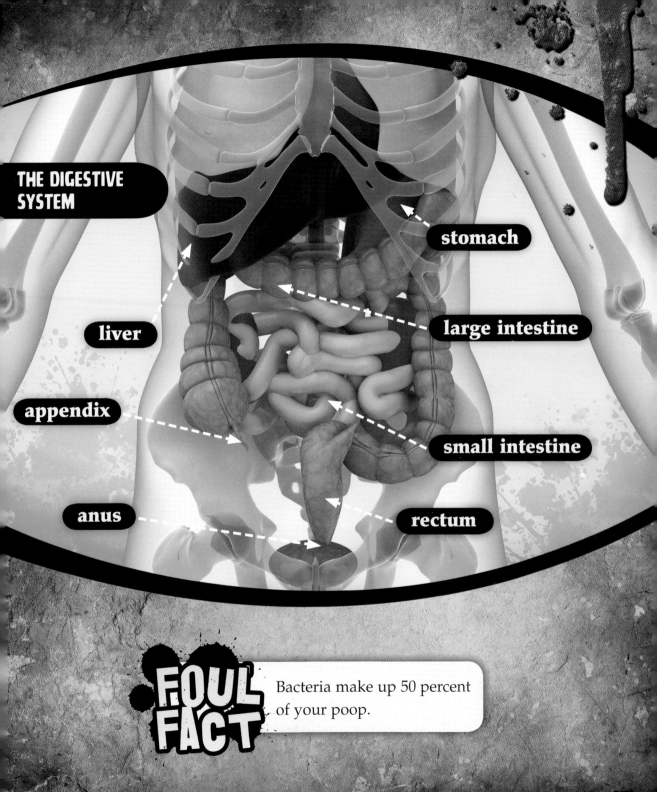

stomach

liver

large intestine

appendix

small intestine

anus

rectum

FOUL FACT Bacteria make up 50 percent of your poop.

WORKING UP A SWEAT

Sweating is another gross body function. But sweating is your body's way of controlling your temperature. The hotter you are, the more you sweat. When air moves across the sweat, the water **evaporates**. The evaporation cools you off.

Sweat is made by hollow tubes of cells called sweat glands. The average person has more than 2.6 million sweat glands. Most sweat glands end in holes in your skin called pores. The fluid that leaks out of these glands is mostly water and salt. That's why your skin tastes salty after your sweat has evaporated.

A person who lives in a hot climate will sweat out 4 to 6 pints (2 to 3 liters) of liquid per hour.

evaporate: to change from a liquid into a gas

A different type of sweat gland is found in your armpits and crotch. The sweat that trickles out of these glands is thicker than the sweat on your forehead. Armpit sweat also has a milky, yellowish color.

Skin bacteria love to snack on this thick sweat. When bacteria eat, they release gases. And, as we discovered with farts and poop, bacteria gases can make things smell a little funky.

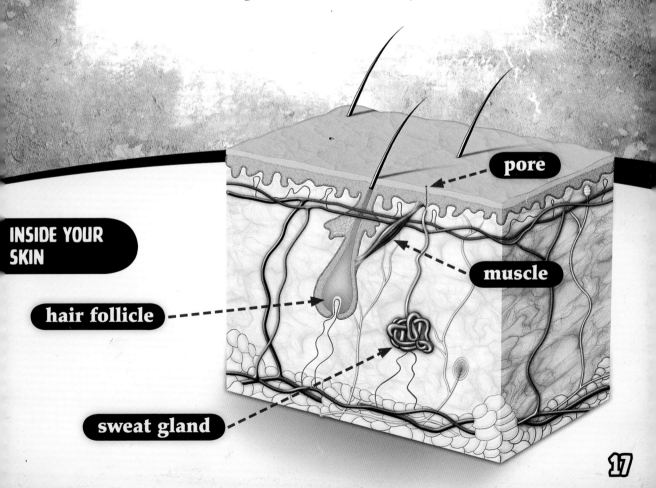

INSIDE YOUR SKIN

pore

muscle

hair follicle

sweat gland

PUS POWER

Sometimes your cuts and scrapes might ooze a watery liquid. That yellowish goop is not sweat. It's pus. Pus forms when a cut, scrape, or other wound gets infected with bacteria.

Oozing pus might be nasty, but it shows that your **immune system** is working. One type of cell in your immune system, called a neutrophil (NEW-truh-fil), finds chemicals made by bacteria. The neutrophils go after the bacteria and eat them. After awhile, each neutrophil explodes. The dead neutrophil plus the bacteria it digested spill out of the wound. And that's what we call pus!

immune system: the part of the body that protects against germs and diseases

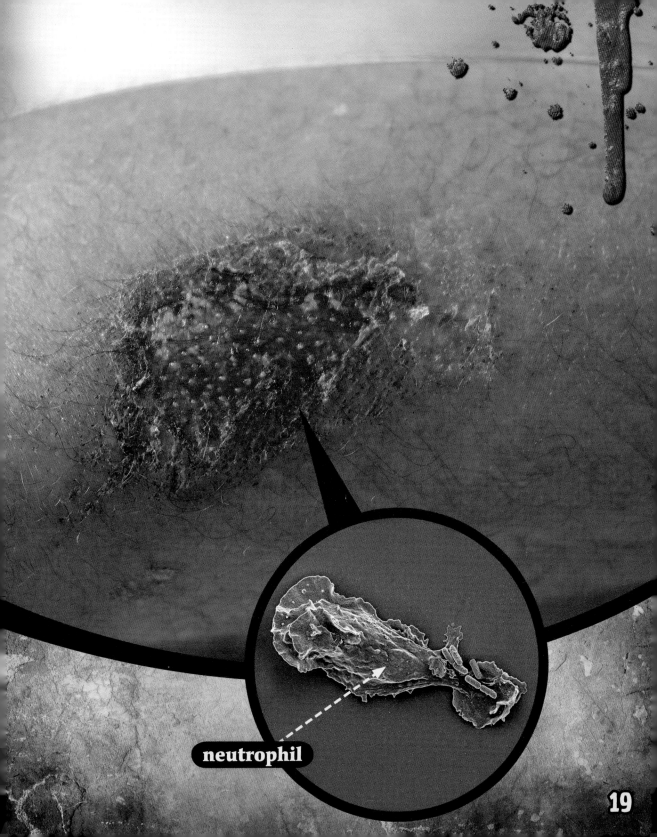

neutrophil

SNOT A SNEEZE

Snot is another slippery, slimy liquid your body makes. Snot, or mucus, is made of water, salt, and chemicals that make it thick and gooey. The skin and hairs inside your nose are totally covered in mucus. Nose hairs and snot work together to trap germs, dirt, and other foreign things that get into your nose. Without snot, a lot of nasty stuff would get sucked down into your lungs.

Most of the time, the snot stew just slips down the back of your throat and into your stomach. But sometimes something big, like a piece of pollen, gets inside your nose and tickles the lining. That's when your brain says, "Enough! Get this stuff out of here." And without you even knowing, your brain tells your body to take a deep breath. Then you sneeze snot and the offending junk out at amazing speed. A snot rocket can shoot out of your nose at around 100 miles (161 kilometers) per hour!

You swallow about 1 quart (1 liter) of snot every day.

BOOGER TRAPS

The snot you don't blast out or swallow dries up. Now you have a nose full of boogers. These flakes are filled with all the strange things you've breathed in. Little bugs, dust, pollen, sand, smoke, and bacteria are all trapped in these delightful, crusty lumps.

COUGH IT UP

Your nose isn't the only place mucus is made. In fact, everything from your nose to your lungs is covered in mucus. The mucus traps bacteria and dust you breathe in. Mucus that's coughed out of your lungs is called phlegm (FLEM). You cough for pretty much the same reason you sneeze. Here's how it works:

1 Something, like a bit of dust, tickles your airway.

2 Your brain reacts quickly. It sends out signals, telling your body to take a big breath.

3 Then your brain tells your **diaphragm** and abdominal muscles to push up on your lungs.

4 This squeeze causes the air to rush out of your lungs. The air blows out of your mouth along with the dust.

diaphragm: a sheet of muscle below your ribs

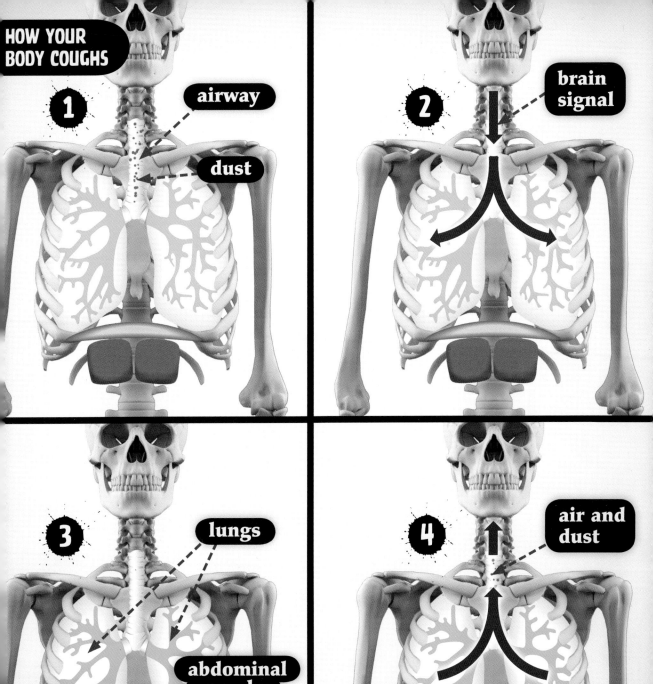

HOW YOUR BODY COUGHS

1 airway

dust

2 brain signal

3 lungs

abdominal muscles

diaphragm

4 air and dust

23

Coughing fits are fairly common when you have a cold. Your body is trying to get rid of whatever is making you sick. Coughing clears your breathing tube right up! But it doesn't make the guy sitting next to you very happy. That's because the phlegm you're spewing contains germs.

Colds are caused by viruses. When you cough and sneeze, virus germs come flying out in droplets of snot and spit. When people around you breathe in the droplets, they get infected with the virus too. So cover your mouth and nose when your body starts spewing snot and spit. And wash your hands to keep globs of germy goo from spreading.

About 3,000 droplets of spit shoot out of your mouth during a single cough.

STICKY EARS

Snot and phlegm stop junk from reaching your lungs. Earwax keeps nasties out of your ears. Earwax is made by glands in your ears that are similar to sweat glands. But instead of oozing watery sweat, they ooze thick, sticky wax. Each of your ears has between 1,000 and 2,000 glands. And they make new wax every day. The new wax pushes out the old wax and anything the wax has trapped in it. In time, the older wax dries up and falls out of your ears.

But earwax does more than trap bugs and dirt. It also keeps the eardrum soft and waterproof. Scientists have found that earwax can kill some types of bacteria too.

earwax magnified
about 160 times

Everyone's earwax is slightly different. Earwax can be wet or dry. Depending on what's trapped in the earwax, it can be different colors too. Earwax can range from golden yellow to grungy gray.

NASTY BUT NICE

No matter how you slice it, your body produces slimy, stinky, crusty stuff for a reason. Most of the time, that reason is to protect you from things that could make you sick. Vomiting gets rid of foreign things in your stomach. Spit, phlegm, and snot keep dirt out of your airways. And earwax makes sure bugs don't get into your ears. You pee and poop to get rid of waste. Your body farts and burps out the gases it doesn't need. Even the yellowish liquid seeping from your wounds has a purpose. These functions may seem nasty, but you really couldn't live without them.

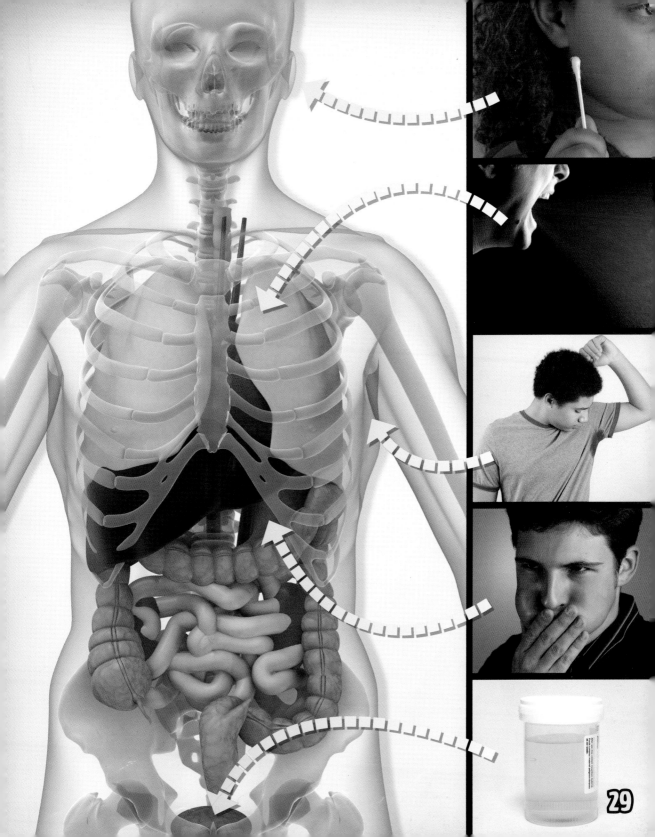

GLOSSARY

chemoreceptor (kee-moh-ree-SEP-tuhr)—a cell that is activated by chemicals; some chemoreceptors tell the brain if poisons are in the body

diaphragm (DYE-uh-fram)—the wall of muscle between your chest and abdomen

digest (dye-JEST)—to break down food so that it can be absorbed into the blood and used by the body

esophagus (i-SAH-fuh-guhss)—the tube that carries food from the mouth to the stomach; muscles in the esophagus push food into the stomach

evaporate (i-VA-puh-rayt)—to change from a liquid into a vapor or a gas

immune system (i-MYOON SISS-tuhm)—the part of the body that protects against germs and diseases

microorganism (mye-kro-OR-gan-iz-um)—a living thing too small to be seen without a microscope

nutrient (NOO-tree-uhnt)—a substance needed by a living thing to stay healthy

pigment (PIG-muhnt)—a substance that gives color to something

READ MORE

Calabresi, Linda. *Human Body*. Insiders. New York: Simon & Schuster Books for Young Readers, 2007.

Royston, Angela. *Ooze and Goo*. Disgusting Body Facts. Chicago: Raintree, 2010.

Silverstein, Alvin, Virginia Silverstein, and Laura Silverstein Nunn. *Snot, Poop, Vomit, and More: The Yucky Body Book*. Yucky Science. Berkeley Heights, N.J.: Enslow Publishers, 2010.

Siy, Alexandra, and Dennis Kunkel. *Sneeze!* Watertown, Mass.: Charlesbridge, 2007.

INTERNET SITES

FactHound offers a safe, fun way to find Internet sites related to this book. All of the sites on FactHound have been researched by our staff.

Here's all you do:

Visit *www.facthound.com*

FactHound will fetch the best sites for you!

INDEX